Christmas Story

by Richard Sills

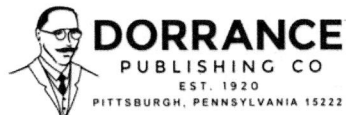

DORRANCE
PUBLISHING CO
EST. 1920
PITTSBURGH, PENNSYLVANIA 15222

Dorrance Publishing Co
701 Smithfield Street
Pittsburgh, PA 15222
Visit our website at *www.dorrancebookstore.com*

ISBN: 978-1-4809-1117-8
eISBN 978-1-4809-1439-1

To: Bettie-Julia

On the night before Christmas,

There was not a sound,

Nothing moving or stirring,

No noise all around.

The candles were lit by the bedside for light,

And only the reindeer flew through the night.

At four in the morning, there was such a clatter

That I jumped out of my bed to see what was the matter.

And there in his clothes of red and of white,

I saw a fat, old, jolly elf who laughed with delight.

"Ho, ho, ho," he laughed, I'll give him a glowing yo-yo."

And he laughed, and he laughed,

and it was then that I knew:

It must be Saint Nicholas; he was long overdue.

"Saint Nick," I asked. "Are you real?"

And he laughed, and he laughed; his warmth I could feel.

"Yes, my friend," he said.

"I'm as real as a reindeer is on a sled.

And to prove I'm real, too, I'll treat you for a ride.

Through the night stars we will glide.

I'll show you tonight

The stops I make all through my dark flight.

But hurry, hurry, hurry if you want to go,

For it is just beginning again to snow!"

And I looked out at my lawn,

And, lo and behold, there was just beginning a storm.

So I said to Saint Nick, "I'd love to go.

I'll get my coat on quick, ho, ho."

We crammed into the fireplace,

And we went up in a race.

And there on the roof I could see

The reindeer were as ready as we.

We climbed on the sled,

And up, up we went as we said,

"MERRY CHRISTMAS!

MERRY CHRISTMAS TO ALL

on this joyous night!"

As we flew through the stars,

it was quite a sight.

The first place we came upon

Was a little house as small as a fawn.

And out from his bag,

Santa pulled out a rag.

It was red,

And he rubbed it in his hands as he said,

"It is a miracle. It is made of love,

And it brings to its holder a gentle, white dove."

Carefully, he slipped it in the chimney and became

As small as a doll,

And down and down he did fall.

When he came out again,

He wiggled, jiggled, and laughed with a grin,

"Roger, the seagull will be in the wind."

And then, like a toy balloon, he blew up once again

To his fat, old, jolly self.

Such a man, I felt, full of wealth,

His smile was as rich as an earl's,

And his teeth shone like pearls.

His hair flowed like silk, and his clothes were adorned

With ornaments and jewels which were well worn.

When he laughed, he seemed to enjoy

The simple laughter of a child with a toy.

Was he old? Or was he young?

This is a mystery I must think upon.

For, though it is written that he was long ago,

I never saw him once, and that I did know.

But here in my age, now I see

Him sitting right next to me.

It gives me a thought. It gives me a doubt

As to what this whole world is really about.

For, here beside me,

I would like to sit on his knee

And ask him for a present, just for me.

And then, as a surprise,

He turned his eyes up to the skies.

"Yes," he laughed, "I have a nice present for thee.

And when you unwrap it, think kindly of me."

"Oh boy, Saint Nick," I said.

"Tell me what it is and send me to bed!"

"No, no, not yet," he spoke,

With a twinkle of laughter in his throat.

"The dawn is not here,

And you ought to know by now

You can't open up Christmas presents

Till the morning bell rings.

So just relax and enjoy

The gifts I am giving to all good girls and boys."

Through the night

We went, lit by Rudolph's bright light.

For his nose, like the sun,

Shown a path of fun.

And we were warm, too,

Though the snow made us shiver as we flew.

And songs we sang, too:

We sang all the Christmas songs you normally sing;

We sang all the songs that church bells ring.

And after all the singing

And work was all done,

We drank a toast to Christmas

With cold eggnog and hot biscuits,

Which he pulled out from his bag

With a wink and a tag.

Yes, the flight,

It lasted all night.

And at dawn I went down the chimney

Feeling quite frisky.

I could still hear Santa call,

"MERRY CHRISTMAS, MERRY CHRISTMAS,

MERRY CHRISTMAS TO ALL!"

But I, in my heart, did not know what to say,

Still wondering what he'd given me

this fine Christmas day.

It was early in the morning,

And I was just yawning.

I was in bed,

Still cold when I said,

"Let's see what Santa's brought us for Christmas, dear.

Wake up. Wake up.

It's Christmas."

And as she turned 'round for a kiss,

I was still yawning and she missed.

"You're freezing," she screamed.

"What have you been doing, my dream?"

"I've been with Santa tonight,

With him on his dark, merry flight."

She shook her head

And went back to bed.

"But,

Wake up!"

And I made my hands like a cup.

"Up, up!"

And the snow on my head

Dripped into my hands, which were red.

This time she got up, all right,

In the snow so white,

With cold water

And snow dripping down from her.

And finally she rose

And put on her beautiful clothes.

It was wonderful to see,

Her as slim as could be.

And I said to myself, "Oh, what a beauty,

Just for me."

And when we went
down the stairs,
Lo and behold,
our children were there,
Talking and laughing
and waiting so fair,
Just for us to appear.
And I said, "All you dears,
I bet you knew all along
Santa was here.

But I didn't, you know,
Yet now I know he's
as real as the snow
On that cold winter's night.
I know now
Santa's in flight."

And then I went to the tree

And looked for a present for me.

But there was nothing there for me,

Nothing by the tree

And nothing by the stockings hung by the chimney.

There was nothing, nothing, there for me.

Needless to say, I felt quite blue

While the children laughed and played, too.

Then my wife came to me and sat

On my lap.

"A child will be my gift to you,

So please don't be blue.

I give you life and love, too."

"Oh, thank you, thank you, Santa," I said.

And faintly, I swear I could hear

Him laughing, and his tiny elves and reindeer.

"Oh, thank you! What a merry Christmas.

A merry, merry Christmas

For me this year."